SHE'S HOME

Emile

I STARE AT MY PHONE IN SHOCK.

A gorgeous pair of bright baby blues stare back at me. Look. There's that familiar crooked half-smile that barely hides the most adorable gap between her front teeth. Sure, she could've worn braces back when she was a kid, but she had liked the space so she kept it.

It was a good call.

Felicity always had the whole innocent thing going on: bouncy blonde curls, big blue eyes, curves to kill for. The gap was just the icing on the cake. Five years later, and she looks as sweet—and delicious—as ever.

She's wearing a tight tank in the photo, with cleavage deeper than the grand canyon. An oversized red, white, and blue flannel hangs on her frame, rolled

1

up to her elbows as if admitting that—even in Salem, Massachusetts—the early summer weather means it's hotter than she likes. And those jeans... the shot stops at her hips, her body turned to the camera, but I don't have to see it to know that the dark denim jeans are molded to her luscious ass.

I swallow a groan at just the memory of it.

God, I miss that ass.

Finally tearing my gaze away from her infectious smile, I stare at the caption posted below the picture. I read it for the third time, trying to make sense of it:

Join us at good ol' Salem High to celebrate the Fourth! We'll have fireworks at dusk (around 9:15 but the party starts way before that). There will be music, local food trucks, face-painting, and a bounce house for the kiddies, capped off with a grand finale for the ages. Food, Fireworks, & Freedom—you can't go wrong!

That's the ad for the festival. Beneath it, Felicity's added a paragraph of her own:

** hey guys! I'm going to be at the 4th of July festival doing face-painting with Kris. All proceeds will go to Salem High's arts and music program and since Kris is letting me stay with her while I find a place of my own in town, I want to see all of my Salem friends stop by to support us! Don't make me feel like I should return to Jersey, lol.

It takes a couple of seconds for it to sink in. Not the first part. Anyone who grew up in Salem knows that the high school throws a huge party for Independence

WHEN SPARKS FLY

A STEAMY 4TH OF JULY NOVELLA

SARAH SPADE

Day. You could go to the big event over at the Derby Wharf, but that's more for tourists. Locals know that the fireworks at Salem High are a treat even if they're not an explosion over open water, plus the chance to support the kids makes it more of a community thing. I stopped going a couple of years ago. I still remember it fondly.

Hearing that Felicity will be there with her sister, Kris? Using her fancy Mason Gross art degree to decorate little kid's faces? *That* doesn't make sense. Last I knew, she was living in New Jersey, commuting in to Manhattan, working at some high end gallery.

She swore to me... what? Almost three years ago now? Yeah. Three years ago in May. She swore to me that she would never move back to Salem. She hadn't just left me behind when she went off to Rutgers. She shook the cobwebs of Salem off of her boots before heading down the East Coast. I haven't spoken to her since.

Not because I didn't want to. Felicity is the one who decided that a clean split was what we needed. It just about killed me to respect that. I had no choice, though. It's my fault and I've had years to accept that.

If it wasn't for me being so young and stupid and insisting that we took that fucking "break" in the first place, Felicity might have come back to me when she graduated.

Only she didn't.

Or did she?

Shit.

I read the caption again.

...while I find a place of my own in town, I want to see all of my Salem friends stop by to support us! Don't make me feel like I should return to Jersey, lol...

I'll be damned.

Felicity Houston is back in Salem and, until this post popped up on my newsfeed, I had no clue.

And I should. I'm not proud to admit it, but I've been stalking Felicity ever since she told me that she'd moved on without me. Not stalking *stalking* because I haven't followed her to her apartment in Avenel or anything; I know it makes me seem a little bit of a wacko that I even try to make that distinction. Her social media, though? I check it as often as I check mine.

There's no way that Felicity posted about moving home and I missed it. Just in case, I click her profile pic, scrolling down her entire feed. There's nothing out of the ordinary there. A selfie here, a picture of a sunset, a meme that features that sad-looking cat—

Wait.

"You may not always end up where you thought you were going, but you will always end up where you are meant to be..."

I remember this. One of those inspirational quotes

4

on a pale pink background with a butterfly flapping in the distance.

She posted it more than a month ago. I had scrolled right on by it because—and, okay, this sounds even worse—I was only really checking her pictures. So long as it wasn't Felicity with some dude, it didn't even register.

Even though we broke up for good the summer after high school graduation, and we both decided it was over, I realized too late that I gave up the best thing I ever had. So I've spent the last couple of years obsessively checking her page, dreading the moment that her status would change from **single** to **in a relationship**. It hasn't happened yet, not in the last two years that I've been watching, so I started to keep an eye out for her posting pics of her with any other guy.

That hasn't happened, either. All along it's given me some hope that, maybe, one day I might get another chance at her. I haven't even looked at another woman since I accepted that Felicity—my girlfriend all through high school, the one I stupidly let get away—was the only one I really wanted. So I watched, and waited, and I fucking hoped that this New York gig wouldn't work out.

Apparently, though, I'm a pretty shit stalker. Somehow, some way, it hasn't worked out. And I'm just finding out now.

"...*where you are meant to be...*"

Felicity is meant to be in Salem.

She's meant to be with me.

I run my thumb across the screen, scrolling all the way to the top. I caress her cheek, then read the first line again.

Join us at good ol' Salem High to celebrate the Fourth.

Hmm. It's not exactly stalking if I show up at the festival to see fireworks, maybe chow down on a hot dog or two, then casually bump into Felicity as if I had no clue she was there, is it?

I pause, cock my head, close the app and slip my phone into the back pocket of my jeans. Well... *yeah*. I guess it *is* stalking.

Too bad that that's not going to be enough to stop me.

"HEY, MA. WHATCHA DOIN'?"

My mother tucks a strand of short brown hair behind her ear as she bows over a tray of freshly iced cupcakes. Each one is topped with a generous mound of white icing, alternating red and blue jimmies, and a paper American flag wrapped around a toothpick stuck in the top. Every year since Zack first enrolled at Salem High, she makes an offering for every fundraiser the school hosts. I graduated five years ago and she still does it, every holiday, all year-round.

This year, though, she pledged to make the cupcakes but she wasn't going to be able to work the bake sale stand like she normally did. Dad had tickets to a concert in Boston for the pair of them and she asked me last week to take her place. Since I could think of a hundred other things I could be doing on the Fourth—since I was getting a long weekend out of it and didn't have to go back to work until Monday, four days later—I told her to ask Zack.

My brother couldn't. He didn't want to leave his pregnant wife alone with their neurotic cat. Salem—they actually named their cat that—hated loud noises and they were going to stay home and keep him calm during the explosion of fireworks around town.

Now? Now I'm glad that Zack came up with the wussiest excuse ever.

I might have gone to Salem State U, but I've gotten some good use out of my marketing degree since I graduated last spring. I work full-time as a social marketing assistant for a local retail chain, analyzing their business trends, focusing on their brand and how it's perceived (specifically on social media), and I do off-site events to build their brand awareness. It's an entry level position, with room to grow; considering I just scraped by to earn my degree, I'm grateful for it. With the stress of Zack's accident and his two-year-long coma weighing on me during the final year and a half of my program, it was a surprise I graduated at all. I like my job and I'm damn good at it.

I spend the car ride over to my parents' house working out a plan to market myself. I know exactly how to do it, too. Emile Banks, perfect son, the kid who would drop whatever plans he has for the Fourth of July to do whatever his mother asks of him. So I didn't have any worthwhile plans for the holiday before I saw Felicity's post. Mom needs me, so here I am.

Only one problem.

I'm a class-A marketer, a man who can sell anything. But my mom? She's not buying it.

Her brows are furrowed, a twinkle gleaming in her dark brown eyes. She purses her lips. "Cut the shit, Emile, honey. What do you want?"

Even though I'm caught, I have to admit that it's still nice to see that look on her face again. After Zack's accident, Mom always wore a pinched expression, expecting at any moment that the phone would ring and the doctors would tell her that he was never coming out of his coma. She held out hope—we all did, my mother, my father, and me—that he'd wake up eventually. When he shockingly did last November, it was like things could finally get back to normal.

Mom looking at me like she knows I'm full of shit is as normal as it could be.

I smile. "Nothing. Honest."

Her bark of laughter has my innocent grin slipping

off my face. "Honest? Is that 'nothing, honest' like the time your brother caught you and Felicity in our hot tub? Or 'nothing, honest' like how you dropped your brother off at a friend's house when he was only weeks out of a coma? Oh, baby, I love you, but I stopped believing your stories when you were about twelve."

She's got a point. I might have been known to stretch the truth a little bit sometimes while I was growing up. But, hell, I'm twenty-three now. Even if I had no clue that Mom knew about that time with Felicity when we were both sixteen, I only ever lied to protect her. There are just some things a mother doesn't need to know about her boys.

My smile turns sneaky. She wants to hear the truth? I can do that. "Zack didn't go to a friend's house. He was running straight to Dani. How much you want to bet that was the night he knocked her up?"

"And you tell me that now." Mom finishes putting the last cupcake in the tupperware container before rolling her eyes up to the heavens. She hasn't done that in ages, either. "I guess it was worth it, though. I'm getting my first grandbaby out of it."

True. Dani, Zack's new wife, is already six months along, due in the beginning of October. Zack must've have some real potent swimmers after being asleep for all that time, courtesy of the damn bus that plowed him right off of his motorcycle. Not even two months into their relationship and he had knocked her up.

Of course, once I heard the news, I couldn't stop myself from wondering what it would be like if me and Felicity ever had kids. I always pushed the thought out of my head, since I figured it was impossible; I'm pretty proud of my dick, but as big as it is, no way in hell could it reach to New Jersey.

And it wasn't like I could move. I might have, but then Zack got into his accident, and it would've been a real shitty thing to leave him and my parents alone while he was in the coma. Once he was awake again, there was Zack's rehab, his sudden relationship with Danielle, and a whirlwind wedding. I was best man. Now she's pregnant and my little niece/nephew is on the way. Plus, there's my job.

I couldn't leave Salem.

I could've made a trip to tell her how I feel, but what would that have done? She's the one who refused to take me back when I called her, basically begging her for a second chance. I love her—I still do—but that woman doesn't change her mind once she sets it. With my luck, Felicity would've tossed me on my ass outside of her apartment.

Now I guess it's a good thing I waited after all. Felicity is back.

She's home.

And I can't wait to show her how much I've missed her.

"Are those the cupcakes for the bake sale?"

"They were supposed to be," Mom says dryly, loading the cupcakes into a big, plastic tupperware container perched next to her on the counter. "I ran out of time to drop them off myself and Lizzie is manning the stand by herself this year. She couldn't stop by to pick them up once I got them done. Since you didn't want to help me, I told your brother he could have them if Dani wants them."

That's my mom. Always trying to fatten us all up while never missing a step when it comes to sending me on a guilt trip.

Barbara Banks is a pro. If I hadn't already figured I could use the cupcakes to my advantage, her last comment alone would've been enough to have me hawking baked goods next to Lizzie.

If this works out, I'll get good son brownie points as well as another shot at Felicity Houston. That's a win-win in my books.

But, first, I've got to get my hands on that tupperware.

"That's actually why I'm here. I don't have time to stay and sell them, but I can at least drop them off. Half of Salem will be disappointed if your cupcakes aren't there."

Mom's eyebrows wing up. And, okay, I might've laid it on a little thick there.

Oh, well.

Whatever works.

She purses her lips. "Really? Out of the kindness of your heart?"

My heart's one part of me that's involved. My dick's another.

Definitely not telling Mom that, though.

I give her my best innocent grin. "You betcha."

Mom doesn't say anything. She just reaches inside of the container and pulls out two cupcakes, one in each hand. When she sees me watching her curiously, she says, "I'm saving these for Dani."

"So it's okay if I take the rest of the cupcakes over to Salem High for you?" I ask.

I need them. I might not have talked to Felicity since she told me that we were through for good, but I'm willing to bet she still knows me better than most. After my mother, she was the best at looking past my bullshit. If I just show up, she'll suspect something. The cupcakes give me a reason.

Mom knows I'm up to something. I know she does. But she shrugs.

"If you really want to. I would appreciate it."

"Then consider it done."

"Mm." She shakes her head, grabbing the lid to the tupperware. It goes on with a snap. "Emile?"

"Yeah?"

"Do me a favor."

"Anything for you, ma."

"Tell Felicity I said hi when you see her, okay?"

Mom glances up. She takes one look at my dumb-founded face and grins knowingly before picking up the tupperware full of cupcakes and placing them on the table in front of me. She stops to tap my cheek lightly, laughing as she heads out of the kitchen.

You know? I had to get it from somewhere, right?

I should've been expecting that.

2

CATCHING UP

Felicity

THE LAST TIME I WAS AT SALEM HIGH, I WAS STILL A student here.

Now? Now I'm a teacher—well, I'm gonna be.

My sister Kris teaches music and is in charge of the chorus. When the school was looking for someone to take over as an art instructor, she immediately thought of me. I got my degree in art, not education, but she pointed out that I could get the job if I passed the MTEL and got a preliminary teaching license.

I flew up last month to interview with the principal, then the superintendent. Provided I have my preliminary teaching license before the school year started, I got the job.

Of course, that meant I had to move back to Salem.

That was almost a dealbreaker. I swore up and down that I was never coming back. It had good memories and bad, and I missed my family like crazy while I lived in New Jersey, but the distance did something to soothe my broken heart.

Because Emile? The boy I loved and lost? He still lives in Salem.

In the end, though, Kris talked me into it. She knew I wasn't happy working at the gallery anymore and while art is my passion, it doesn't pay the greatest. Commuting into Manhattan six days a week—plus all of my student loans starting to be due—was killing my finances. I could barely afford my one-room apartment in Avenel.

Teachers might not make much, but it's better than what I did have. Plus, Kris told me that I can stay with her, her husband, and my nieces rent-free while I try to find a place of my own that I can afford. There was no reason not to take the job. I have Kris to thank for kicking me in the ass and gutting my butt in gear.

My sister is awesome.

She's also missing.

We're supposed to be running the face-painting stand together. I'm taking care of the kids in the seat while she keeps the ones waiting in line occupied. For most of the afternoon the line was almost out of control—we're definitely a big hit at the festival, our cash box bursting with all of the donations we've received for the Arts program.

Once it started to wind down a little, once the sun began to go down, Kris left me with the few stragglers still waiting for me to draw hearts and stars and fireworks on their adorable cheeks. Her husband Dave had picked out a great spot to see the fireworks show and she went to meet him and her twin girls so that she didn't miss any of it.

I don't really mind. They promised I could share their blanket with them when I shut our stand down and, since it's not like I came here with anyone else, I said sure.

Having been gone for the last five years, I've lost touch with a lot of people I used to know. Sure, we're friends on social media, sharing each others' posts, liking each others' comments, but most of them are doing their own thing.

That's why I just about have a heart attack when I hear a very familiar voice call out to me—

"Felicity? Holy shit. Is that you?"

It's a good thing I had already finished up with the last kid otherwise I might've drawn a line of paint across her cheek, I jumped so high. My heart starts going a mile a minute. I take a second to calm down, then turn.

I immediately freeze.

Emile.

It's Emile.

Of course it is.

I should've recognized that voice immediately. Maybe, if I had, I could've bolted through the face-painting stand, leapt over the fence surrounding the field, and been halfway back to Jersey before I had to face Emile again.

Too late.

My jaw drops. I'm gaping. I'm pretty sure I'm gaping.

This can't be Emile, can it?

I've always thought he was cute. From the time I was ten and he was my first crush, I always thought Emile was the cutest boy in the neighborhood. Of course, we both had our awkward stages, but he never lost any of his humor or his charm. By the time he went through puberty, coming out on the other side as a good-looking teen with shaggy dark brown hair, dark eyes, and a mischievous smile, all the girls at school thought he was hot. He was mine and I made sure they all knew it, but he was still eye candy all around.

The man standing across from me is drop dead sexy.

Has he always been this tall? He's got almost a whole head on me, and his loose white tee does nothing to hide the guns he's packing beneath his clothes. He's wearing his hair longer than he used to, with this one strand that keeps flopping in front of his face, curling enticingly past his forehead.

The smile he's wearing? Some time in the last five years he's graduated from mischievous to full-on devilish.

Oh, mama. I'm in *trouble*.

"Felicity Houston. I never thought I'd see the day you'd come back to Salem."

I don't know what to say. For one of the first times in my life, I'm entirely at a loss for words. I open my mouth, hoping something calm, cool, and collected will come out, only to be cut off when a tall black woman with the most adorable little boy approaches the face-painting stand.

She's wearing an encouraging smile, shooing her son forward with a gentle push. "Go on, Johnathan. Tell the nice lady what you'd like."

The little boy mumbles something, ducks his head, then scurries to hide behind his mother.

She laughs. "He's a little shy. He wanted to know if you're still painting faces. He didn't want to ask before when his sister was getting hers done, but he really wants a star."

I glance over at Emile. He gestures with his chin to the cupcake-filled tupperware container in his hands. "Let me just go drop these off. Don't go anywhere, okay? We've got some catching up to do."

My heart is thumping wildly. I thought he would

take the chance to escape and get the hell out of here. But he's coming back.

Oh, man, oh, man, *ohman*.

"Sure. I'm just gonna take care of this little man here." My voice sounds so calm, so sure. I deserve a prize. "Johnathan, right? What color star would you like?"

From behind his mother's legs, he pokes his head out. I can tell he's still nervous, but the beginning of a small, shaky grin comes to his face. "A blue one."

"You're in luck. I have plenty of blue paint left. Come on up. Take a seat."

His mother throws me a grateful look. She helps Johnathan get situated on the stool, then steps back while I paint of trio of blue stars on the little boy's cheeks. Taking my time, putting him at ease, I draw the outline in dark blue, fill it in with a shade lighter, then use the darker paint to give it some shadows, some depth. A little white paint to highlight each star and I'm done.

The kid is a pro. He might've been nervous to approach the stand, but he sits still the entire time I paint on him. Just because I'm desperate to escape the stand before Emile comes back doesn't mean I'm not going to do the best I can for Johnathan. His bravery deserves to be rewarded.

I just wish I was half as brave as this little five-year-old .

Johnathan's mother gushes over the design when I'm done. I show Johnathan his image in the mirror and am in turn rewarded with a softly whispered, "Thank you." His mother adds ten dollars to our donation box, and I'm grateful for it, but it's the happiness coming off of the boy when they head off to see the fireworks that makes me feel warm inside.

A moment later, Emile comes strolling back around the front of the stand. The tupperware container is empty now, and the expression on his handsome face tells me that there's no getting out of this without another crack on my already battered heart.

The warmth inside of begins to travel south.

He beams over at me. "You're still here."

As if I could leave. "I am."

"I'm glad." Emile grins. Did I think he couldn't get more handsome? Ugh. I was wrong. "It's, uh, wow. It's so good to see you. I can't believe it. I was just dropping off some cupcakes my mom made for the festival and, shit, here you are."

He moves toward me.

Wait. Do I hug him? You hug old friends, right? What about old lovers? Crap. Too late. I go in for the hug.

Damn it. Bad idea. He smells so delicious, his masculine scent a combination of his soap, his deodorant, and *Emile*. He never wore any cologne when we were together and he doesn't now.

It takes everything I have to let go. It's gotta be close to seventy-five degrees out and, still, I miss his warmth as soon as I back away from him.

Say something, Felicity, and please god don't let it have anything to do with how amazing he looks—

"How have you been? I heard about Zack." Everyone in Salem heard about his brother getting hit by a bus. "If I had known about his accident..."

What? If someone had told me that Emile's older brother had been hit by a bus and, as a result, laid in a coma for almost two years, would I have come back? I'd like to think so. Since Kris kept it from me and Emile didn't feel the need to share, who knows?

I hear the accusation in my voice at the same time as Emile does. He winces. "It was a rough time. I probably could've used a friend, but you know me. I sucked it up and dealt with it."

It's my turn to wince. *Friend.* Is that all I was?

When we were still in school together, he used to tell me I was made only for him.

But then he dumped me.

I step back. If Emile notices, he doesn't say anything. He just lifts one of those big, brawny hands, running it through his effortlessly styled hair. That's the thing about Emile. He never had to try hard. He was sexy and funny and cute all without trying to be.

22

And I realize with a start that my worst suspicions are confirmed. I really do still carry a torch for him.

Crap.

"Zack's doing great. He's married now. His wife is actually gonna have a baby. October." He chuckles. "Halloween baby. Seems about right for those two. They have this weird inside joke about Halloween that none of us get, but that's alright. My bro is happy. Can't ask for more."

I welcome the new direction of the conversation. Good idea, Emile. If we don't talk about the past, then I don't have to acknowledge how you ripped my heart out of my chest, trampled it underneath your sneakers, then went on your merry way. And, alright, what happened to Zack had to have been hell on the entire Banks family, but he's okay now and, suddenly, I feel like the distraught eighteen-year-old girl I had been when Emile—after we'd been together for five years— gave up what we had all because we were going to different schools.

Looking at Emile as dusk begins to fall is almost like staring at the sun during the mid-afternoon. It's super painful, yet I just can't look away. It's almost blinding.

He might have been the one to change the subject, bring up Zack's miraculous recovery, tell me about his new wife.

Wife.

Suddenly, I can't help it. I have to know.

I manage to tear my gaze away from him, turning my attention to the face-painting stand. I close up the box of paints, stick the last paintbrushes into my big cup of dirty water, then ask the only question that's running through my mind.

"Glad to hear it. How... how about you? Married? Kids?"

I hold my breath, trying not to look too relieved when Emile says, "Nope. It's just me."

I glance up at him. The easy smile that had been on his face is replaced by a more heated expression. "Oh. That's... that's nice."

"What about you?"

"Just me, too, I guess. Not really, since I'm staying at Kris's house with her family while I'm apartment-hunting, but that's about it."

"So you're single?"

I shrug. "For now."

I'm not exactly sure what it is that I said. Emile tosses the now-empty tupperware container onto the flat surface next to my paints. I follow the arc of the rubber container, making sure it doesn't knock over any of my paints or the dirty water cup. That's the only reason I miss seeing him move.

He's fast. Really fast. He's got me wrapped up in his arms, stealing my breath with a sizzler of a kiss before I can even react. My mouth was open in surprise and

Emile takes full advantage of it, slipping his tongue inside. He strokes mine with his, before nipping at my bottom lip with his teeth. He's waiting for my reaction.

I melt right into his embrace and kiss him back.

I must have lost my mind.

3

HE'S A HUNGRY MAN

Felicity

EMILE'S THE ONE WHO FINALLY BREAKS THE KISS, rubbing his swollen lip with his thumb; when I kissed him back, I was maybe a little more enthusiastic than I should've been. He doesn't seem to mind, though, from the way his dark eyes seem to light up as he looks down at me.

"I forgot how much I love your taste." Then, as if I don't know exactly what he means, his gaze dips lower, eyeing my shorts. I immediately can guess the direction of his thoughts, even before he adds, "All of your taste. You were delicious, Felicity."

I'm sure Emile means it as a compliment. My mind's thrown back years ago when he discovered just how much pleasure he got out of going down on me.

When I was still in college, I had one guy try to get me to do it with him in my dorm room and just the idea of letting someone else's mouth anywhere near my pussy had me drying up. It's stupid, I know it is, but it just didn't seem *right*.

And that's the last time I even tried to bring a guy back to my room with me.

Emile licks his lips. Bastard. I can already feel my panties going damp, my body preparing itself for him.

Five years later and Emile Banks can have me creaming from one lascivious look. Hell.

He can tell, too. I've never been the best liar, and I guess I've got a tell. Emile knows exactly what I'm thinking. What I'm feeling.

He lunges toward me again. He doesn't go for another kiss like I'm expecting. Instead, he snags my hand, wrapping it securely inside of his. He's not rough and he's not forceful, but he is determined as he pulls on my arm. He starts to lead me away from the face-painting stand.

I let him.

"Did you drive here?" he says, already steering me away from the thick crowd. Somewhere behind us, I hear the announcement that the fireworks will be starting in a few minutes.

"Yes." I'm breathless. I should be stopping him. It's not like I don't know what's on his mind. He might look different, but Emile hasn't changed one bit. I should stop him—instead, I tell him, "I drive a Honda CRV. It's like a SUV, real roomy."

Emile shoots me a look out of the corner of his eye. His lips quirk upward. "Seats fold down?"

I nod.

"Good. I still drive a two-door. This will be much easier in your car. Where did you park?"

This is it. The moment when I can shut down this madness.

I open my mouth, then clamp it closed.

Feeling like the world's biggest idiot, I point out toward the distant trees.

I just hope the orgasm is worth it.

CALL IT A TOUCH OF FATE OR WHAT, I DON'T KNOW, BUT I arrived early to the festival and got confused as to where to park. I ended up on the far side of the lot, past the football field, where there were maybe only three or four other cars. It's on the opposite field from where they plan on setting off the fireworks and, if I planned on watching them from my CRV, I would've had a crappy view.

Of course, that means that there's no one around when I finally lead Emile over to my car. The lot's pretty empty, and the raucous sounds of the families at the festival seem muted here. My car is toward the back, almost hidden by the trees that border it. Night's fallen fast, dusk a memory. The crowd is anxious for the fireworks to start.

With Emile holding tightly to my hand, I've got something else to look forward to.

He smiles in approval when he sees it. "That's perfect, Felicity."

I could still say no. I don't. I spent the five minute dash behind Salem High thinking about Emile, remembering just what he could do with his tongue, and I'm pretty much gushing. My panties are soaking wet. I wouldn't be surprised if I leaked right through to my shorts. If he's really willing to do this, I'm not about to stop him.

His size might, though.

Using my car starter, I unlock the doors and turn the car on. I don't plan on leaving just yet, but I know how easy it is to get overheated when things get hot and heavy in the backseat of a car. A/C, even in Salem, is a must.

As if he's familiar with this kind of car, Emile heads right to the back, popping the hatchback up. He needs my help folding the seats down, grinning in delight when he finds the blanket I keep in my car for emergencies.

I already suspected what was on his agenda. That just proves it. Only...

"This will never work."

"Of course it will. Here, you lay out right here. Let your legs dangle over the seats, and if I squeeze down on the floor, your pussy will be right where it needs to be! I can get my taste and we'll both be fucking ecstatic."

My pussy clenches, aching for what he's offering me. He wants to taste me? Maybe I've lost my mind, but I want him to do it probably more than he does.

Doesn't change the fact that his shoulders are wide and my car's only so big.

I shake my head. "You won't fit."

"Never understand a hungry man. I'm starving, Felicity. If I have to fold myself up to fit down here, I'll do it. Now you just lay back. I'll take care of these."

My brain is a haze of lust and *I can't believe this is happening.* When he says 'these', I don't know what he means until he boldly reaches out, his focus on my shorts.

I feel the edge of his hands caressing my belly, his fingers hovering right above the button.

"One more chance to stop this before I start," he murmurs.

He waits.

I close my mouth and jut my chin out, daring him to continue.

Emile lets out a rush of air, reaching for the button in the next heartbeat. He makes quick work of my shorts, instructing me to lift my foot and step out of them so that he can remove them. He tosses them in the back. My panties are next. Once I'm half-naked, I scramble into the back of my car, closing the hatchback behind me before I sprawl out on my emergency blanket and eagerly flop onto my back.

It takes Emile a few tense moments to climb in through the front and wedge his body on the floor like he said he would. He fits, too. Just barely, but he fits. My legs are spread, my open pussy inches away from him.

Our eyes lock.

The dashboard glow and the interior lights help me see him. Emile wasn't kidding. He looks absolutely famished and he's eyeing me like I'm his favorite meal.

I expect him to go right to town the instant he's got me naked from the waist down. He doesn't. Instead, he motions for me to lift my ass, gently easing the blanket out from underneath me. The plastic on the back of the seats is kinda lumpy and a little warm. It's manageable, especially after I reposition myself, but I don't understand why he took the blanket.

Then he hands it to me.

Huh? "What's this for?"

"Privacy. I plan on taking my time with this and, if anyone peeks inside the car, you can pretend you're resting. Make sure my head's covered once I get in position, okay?"

So we're really doing this, aren't we? Out in the

open too, just the way I like it. He remembers. Just enough kink to make this more exciting for me, but with a back-up plan in case we're caught.

Holy shit, it's like old times again.

That shouldn't make my half as happy as it does.

"Felicity. Blanket. Otherwise I'm gonna start and I won't care if anyone sees."

I will. It's one thing to experience the risk. It's another to get caught having oral sex in the backseat of my SUV on school property—especially when I'm going to be working here come fall. Pulling myself up to my elbows, I snatch the blanket and shake it out. Just before I cover Emile, I say, "But don't you need to see?"

"I've been dreaming about this pussy for years. Every inch of it is burned in my memory. I don't need to see it to make this good for you."

I shiver at the promise and the heat in his words. He's dead serious. His big body wedged against the floor of the car, he's staring at me like the starving man he claimed to be. If I don't cover him and quick, I have no doubt he'll do exactly what he said.

Flipping the length of the blanket with my wrist, I manage to cover my body from the tits down, hiding the bulge that is Emile. As soon as he maneuvers his body lower, his hot breath warming my inner folds as he lowers his mouth to it, I can hardly tell that he's there. He could've been a pillow or luggage. No one needs to know he's a man.

Right as I get the blanket settled the way Emile wants, I hear the beginning of the Independence Day fireworks start to go off. Even at this distance, they're loud as anything, and I'm so distracted by the *hiss*, *booms* that I miss it when Emile lowers his mouth.

With fireworks on my mind, the only words I have for that first swipe of his tongue is explosive.

Emile has never shied away from anything ever. He always goes for what he wants; it's why his kiss might've taken me by surprise, but it wasn't actually *un*expected. Now that he has me right where he wanted me, he doesn't hesitate.

He dives right in.

He doesn't rush, though. He's never been selfish in that way. He takes his time, driving me crazy, making me squirm as he licks and nuzzles and does everything he can to avoid touching my clit.

Then, after what feels like an eternity of pleasurable torture, he sucks it right into his mouth, pulling on it gently, sucking the sensitive bundle with enough force to be my undoing.

I don't fight it.

My orgasm comes crashing over me just as the constant crackling and booming over my head signals the beginning of the grand finale. I see sparks behind my eyes as my toes curl. A squeal escapes me again and I quickly throw my arm over my mouth to muffle it. I doubt anyone can hear me with the cacophony just outside.

Emile lazily licks me one last time before nuzzling my clit again. He's not done yet. I'm torn between wanting to pull him closer and shoving him away. It feels so good, that first burst of pleasure leaving me boneless and limp, but I can feel a buzzing down below that's just too much.

His tongue is magical. I always believed that.

And that's not even the best part of him.

He shifts closer, moving his body so that he isn't cramped down there in an awkward position. At least, that's probably what he wants me to think. I can guess what he's doing. He's testing his reach, trying to figure out just how to angle his lower half so that he can take off his own jeans and lay his body over mine.

God help me, if Emile tries to fuck me, I'm not gonna stop him from doing that, either.

And that's when the silhouette just outside of my back window registers.

4

OFFICER RHODES

Emile

I'm just wiping the last of Felicity's arousal from my lips, my thoughts spinning with just how I'm going to get her to agree to letting me go further than just eating her out, when she suddenly goes stiff as a board. A second later, I hear the *rap-tap-tap*ping against the glass.

I immediately drop back to the floor.

Looks like we've got company.

It comes with the risk of getting it on while out in public. It's something that always excited Felicity, and I learned to love the thrill of it while I was with her. Only her, though. It just didn't give me the same kick when I tried it out with anyone else, probably because

Felicity loved it and most of the other girls I knew were too afraid someone would see what we were doing.

Unless they've got amazing night vision and can see through a blanket, we're fine. No one could say for sure that I just pleasured the hell out of her while trapped between her front and back seats. Maybe they're just lost or need directions or something—

The blanket shifts as Felicity rises up on her elbows, the rest of her staying flat and covered. I hear the whir of the automatic windows going down. And then, "Evening, officer. Is everything okay?"

—or maybe it's a cop.

Shit.

His voice is a rumble, both authoritative and big. He doesn't sound all that old, though, and I'm dying to get a peek at him. "I could ask you the same thing. Miss Houston?"

"That's me."

"I'm Officer Rhodes. I work with Dave."

"Kris's husband. I thought you looked familiar. How are you?"

"Fine, fine. Actually, I'm on patrol tonight, making sure the festival is safe. Your sister mentioned that you seemed to disappear and asked me to keep an eye out for your car. Are you alright, miss? Fireworks are over and nearly everyone is gone."

"Really? I must not have noticed. I was... uh... a little tired after being in the heat all day. I thought I told Kris I was going to lie down for a second. I must've fallen asleep. I'm up now, though, so I guess I'll call her, let her know I'm fine."

"I'd do that. Dave took her and the kids home when you were missing, but she was worried about you. Probably best to let her know." The cop pauses for a moment. "You sure you're okay? It's not the best idea for a pretty girl like you to fall asleep outside on her own."

For his sake, I hope this cop doesn't think because he's on the same force as Felicity's brother-in-law that he has a chance with her. Pretty girl? Try fucking gorgeous, and with a pussy that tastes like liquid gold.

I snort. He wouldn't be laying it on so thick if he knew where my face had been seconds before he interrupted us.

The cop has no clue where I am. Felicity obviously hasn't forgotten. She clamps her knees around my head. I don't know if she means to do this on purpose or if it's a signal for me to keep quiet. Doesn't matter. Her knees pin my ears to my head and I wiggle just enough to get rid of the pressure.

Next thing I know, my face is mere inches away from her open pussy. If I dip my head a little more, her curls will tickle the tip of my nose.

Oh. This is just too perfect.

Above my head, I can make out Felicity still talking to the cop. Something about "Yes, officer" and "My doors were locked, so it's safe" and "No, I haven't been drinking".

I give her one last, leisurely lick up her slit, smiling into her folds when Felicity's legs quiver just enough to rustle the blanket.

She scoots back.

I know she can't go too far. The last thing she wants is the cop to see that she's naked from her waist down so Felicity has to stay under the blanket. But the space she puts between us—maybe three or four inches at the most—is too much for me. I only just got her back in my arms. She needs to stay with me.

I grab her leg, rubbing my pointer finger along the back of her knee. She jerks and the blanket flaps.

We both freeze.

Clear as day, I hear the cop rumble. "Something wrong with your leg, Miss Houston?"

"What? Oh. No, no." Felicity kicks out, getting me right in my side. I grunt, low enough that he won't hear me, but loud enough so that she knows she got me *good*. It takes everything I have not to react other than that. I might be having fun with Felicity, but I don't want to get found by this cop.

That's not the point of it. It never had been. Not for us. It's the rush of *almost* getting caught… that's what had always made it so exciting.

I can feel my cock leaking against my boxers. Talk about being excited. I'm so close, I'm about to go off like one of those rockets out in the field. Kneeling in front of her, my mouth watering for another taste, her pussy right there waiting for me to return to it… if that cop doesn't get the fuck out of here and *soon*, I might lose any chance of getting Felicity to agree to letting me take her all the way.

Lucky for us, the cop runs out of reasons to keep the conversation going. After a few more seconds where he hovers just outside of the vehicle, he reminds Felicity to check in with Kris, wishes her a good night, and stomps away. Without the fireworks booming overhead, I can make out his heavy step, the jingle of his handcuffs against each other. A car door opens, it slams, and an engine revs.

Felicity lets out a sigh of relief before nailing me between the ribs again with her heel.

I grunt.

She scoots away from me, so fast that she's gone before I can recover.

Throwing the blanket off of me, I watch as she snatches her clothes up. Felicity shimmies her panties back on, looking everywhere and anywhere but at me as she starts to pull her shorts on next. In less than a minute, she's fully dressed, running her fingers through her curls as if erasing any sign that, a few minutes ago, I had her writhing and squealing and coming from just my mouth.

She pats her pocket, pulls out her keys.

She's getting ready to leave me.

I don't like that.

"Is that it?" I ask her.

Even in the faint orange glow from the overhead light, I can see it when she swallows the lump in her throat. She turns slowly, tilting her head back so that she's looking me in the eye.

There's sadness there, a little regret, and a whole bunch of determination.

Stubborn.

I *knew* it.

"Yes," she says. I recognize that tone in her voice. It's exactly how she sounded that night on the phone when she told me she was sure that we were through. "That's it, Emile." She swallows roughly. "It was good to see you, but you should go."

I know better than to argue. In the back of my mind, I wonder where I left my mother's tupperware, if only because it's way better than accepting that I gave Felicity one hell of an orgasm and even that wasn't enough for her to come back for more.

So I go.

But 'that's it'?

Yeah.

Not if I have anything to say about it.

———

MAYBE I'M BROKEN. I DON'T KNOW. BUT I TAKE HER stubbornness as a personal challenge.

She wants me. The way I made her squeal, even if she had to muffle it... shit, just how *wet* she was. I know she wants me.

It's a start.

I leave, not wanting to, but knowing that I have to. I won't force her. I'd *never* force anyone, but especially not Felicity. Whatever I have to do to convince her that I'm worth a second shot, I'll do it.

And it all starts with the next morning.

It's a good thing that it's a long holiday weekend. I'd like to think I wouldn't have blown off work to go see Felicity again but, after a restless night where I did nothing but dream about how good her body would feel wrapped around my cock again, I'm not so sure. At least I have three more days to find out.

Because I'm not that much of an asshole, I don't head over to Felicity's sisters' house at the crack of dawn. I manage to wait until it's a more godly hour.

At nine o'clock on the nose, I knock on Kris's door. Someone up there must have been smiling down on me because, when the door swings inward, it's not Kris, her police officer husband, or either of her kids.

It's Felicity.

She's up and she's dressed. Good.

This might just work.

She steps out onto the porch. "Emile? What are you doing here?"

"When you kicked me out of your car last night, you forgot to give me your number."

"I didn't forget." Felicity bites down on her lip. "Besides, I never changed it. If you forgot it, that's not my fault."

I rattle off a string of numbers.

"So you didn't forget," she admits. "You could've called. You didn't have to show up here."

Yes, I did. Because I know Felicity. If she recognized my number, she wouldn't have answered. Here, at her sister's house, I had a better shot at getting her to talk to me.

"Sure, I did. How else was I going to invite you out to have breakfast with me?"

"Breakfast? What? Now?"

I nod. "Why not? I know this great little place on the edge of town. You'd love it."

"I don't think that's a good idea."

For her? Probably not. Me, though? It's the best fucking idea I've had in a long time.

"Why not?"

She shakes her head. "I'm gonna go back inside. Bye, Emile."

My reflexes are pretty quick. I've got my boot jammed between the door and the doorjamb before she can even walk inside and try to shut it all of the way behind her. Swallowing the wince of pain, I arrange my features in the most haughty, cockiest expression I can manage.

"What's the matter? It's just breakfast. Unless you're scared." I wait a beat. "It's fine. Don't worry about it."

When we were kids, using the same exact phrase—*unless you're scared*—always seemed to get to her. One time I said that and she retaliated by going on a ferris wheel ride by herself. Another time, I tricked her into going inside of an abandoned cabin in a local woods. The younger kids liked to pretend it was a witch's cabin, just like *Hocus Pocus*. The older kids used it as a make-out station.

We were thirteen. By then, I was ready to evolve our childhood friendship from playmates to to something more.

We shared our first kiss that day. Then I got greedy. I copped a feel, Felicity retaliated by locking me in one of the cabin's empty closets, and I didn't get out again until she sent Zack to free me.

From that day on, I was sure that Felicity Houston was the perfect girl for me. Sometimes I can't believe that I ever forgot that for even a second.

Even better, she could dish it out as well as she took it. By the time we were in a serious relationship, all she would have to do is say the same thing back at me and, next thing I know, I was doing something that no one with any common sense would be doing.

That's how I ended up buck-naked in my parents' hot tub, trying to explain to Zack that me and Felicity were just sharing a bath while Mom and Dad were away for the weekend.

Unless you're scared... come on, Felicity. Take the bait.

Felicity raises her hand, flipping her long mane of bouncy blonde curls over her shoulder. She furrows her brow, biting her lip. Throwing a quick glance behind her, she seems to come to a decision.

"Wait here," she tells me. "Let me just grab my bag."

Yes!

5

FIRSTS

Felicity

I DON'T KNOW I GET MYSELF IN MESSES LIKE THESE.

As he holds the restaurant door open for me, I decide to blame Emile. Nobody else gets to me like he does. I mean, seriously? A dare? We're not kids anymore. Stealing a glance over at him as I sidle past his muscular body, it's pretty damn obvious that we're not kids anymore.

So what's my excuse?

Ignoring the little voice in the back of my head that says I was looking for any excuse to talk to Emile again, I enter in front of him.

It's a nice place. New. Clean. Opened sometime in the last couple of years, I've never been here before. I like it.

The server is cute. She's slender and trim, with tits that totally fills out her uniform shirt. Her dark hair is cut short in a bob, her hazel eyes sparkling as she comes over to greet us. I feel my already nervous stomach drop, expecting Emile to check her out.

To my surprise, he only has eyes for me. He waits for me to order first before telling the server he'll take the Friday special: two Belgian waffles with fresh strawberries on the side, plus three eggs. When she asks him how he'll take them, I blurt out, "Scrambled," without even thinking about it.

Just like that, the awkwardness I imagined seems to melt away. Five years? What five years? It's like no time has passed at all. Even his mannerisms are so similar to the boy I used to love. He leans back in his seat, crossing his arms over his chest, running his hands through the long strands of hair toward the front whenever he gets antsy. The server comes back with our plates—Emile visibly relaxes when he's got his food in front of him—and I ask for another glass of OJ for Emile before he gets the chance.

He grins, rubbing the back of his neck with the palm of one big hand, then proves how well he remembers my likes when he glances toward the server and adds, "And some blackberry jam, if you guys got some. My girl loves it on her toast."

I let the *my girl* slip past me because I'm willing to bet he only said it for the server's benefit. Emile might not have been checking her out, but he would've had to be blind not to notice how she was blatantly drooling over him. Or maybe he's used to it, I don't know.

He's crazy, though, if he thinks a little oral in the backseat of my CRV means anything.

Then again, this is Emile Banks. Crazy used to be his middle name.

I've got to be careful. If I'm not, who knows what he'll get me to agree to next.

Breakfast is... it's nice. Over waffles, bacon and eggs, and toast, Emile asks me about my new job, then tells me all about his. It's nice to see that he's doing well for himself. I steer the conversation away from what life back in Jersey was like since I'm still feeling the sting of leaving it behind. Moving back to Salem was comfy and cozy and perfect. There is no place like home and I really did miss my family. But the Garden State was my chosen home for so long that I get a little wistful just thinking about it.

Emile gets the hint. Either that or he doesn't want me talking about my time at school. Whatever it is, when I change the subject, bringing up Kris, her husband, and the twins, he lets me. Then it's his turn to give me the details about Zack. Salem gossip only goes so far—my mom is still friends with Emile's mom so that's how I know about it—and it's nice to hear Emile say such nice things about Zack.

Because Zack is ten years older than me and Emile, he was more like another parent than a brother. Growing up, Emile was torn between emulating his older brother and ignoring him. It was another thing we had in common. Kris is eight years older than me. She had already moved out to live with Dave by the time my relationship with Emile was just beginning to get serious, but we still were pretty close. She helped guide me through most of my firsts: first period, first kiss, first time with Emile. Then, when he brought up the idea of the "break" only days before I moved to New Jersey, my first heartbreak.

If she knew I let him dare me into going out to eat breakfast with him, she'd *kill* me.

I push that thought out of my head. It's just breakfast with an old friend. That's all it is.

That's all I can let it be.

And that's when Emile makes an off-handed comment as he's finishing his waffle—

"You know what else I love about this place? The bathrooms are big enough for two."

—and our "friendly" breakfast comes grinding to a massive halt for me.

I feel like there's a tennis ball suddenly lodged in my throat. I had taken a bite of my eggs about a second before he said that and it's nearly impossible to swallow. I force it down, my head racing with the implication.

Not that he's basically propositioning me, especially in a public place. I'd expect no less from any version of Emile. And the public thing? So, yeah, last night wasn't a fluke. When we could get away with it, that's how we always used to be because that's how *I* got off the hardest.

Reckless teen, no care about getting caught. Hell, I'm beginning to think neither of us has matured all that much since that close call with the cop last night nearly had me coming *and* going.

I missed it. All of it.

The rush.

His touch.

The pleasure.

But he isn't mine anymore.

Jesus, Felicity, what are you *doing*?

I should know better. The stories my girlfriends told me about his wild college days, the way he went from adorable teen to this hunk in front of me... I should know better. I've never been to this joint before. How does he know the size of the bathroom? It doesn't take a genius to figure it out.

What we had when we were younger was special. He might have been the one to suggest the "break" that became permanent, but I didn't fight for us, either. And maybe I fell back into our old ways too easily last night when I fell right on my back for him. My bad. But we're not together now. And we weren't together when he visited the bathrooms with someone else.

Knowing that is one thing. Doesn't help me get the idea of Emile leading some faceless chick into a stall and banging it out with her out of my head.

I can't blame him for being Emile. I can't control what—or who—he did in the time since we broke up. I can only control how I react.

I will my hands steady. Once they are, I pick up my coffee, take a sip. Compose myself. And I ask, "Is it always just about sex with you?"

It's an honest question. From the way he kissed me last night to how quickly I was willing to drop my panties for just one swipe of his magical tongue, I can't deny that sex has always been a big thing for us. But that's the problem. In the old days, we had a true relationship. We had similar likes, the same sort of outlook on life, a lot of shared experiences. Sure, sex became intertwined in what we were together, but that was because we learned how to *do* it together.

Emile was my first in so many ways. My first boyfriend, my first lover, my first heartbreak. When he told me that he thought we should split up before I went away to college, I thought my life was over.

It only got worse when I found out that he didn't waste any time in hooking up with some of his new classmates. Apparently "break" meant something different to Emile than it did to me. I tried to call him, tried to understand what he expected of me, but it was like his phone was always off. It wasn't a surprise when I finally heard from him and he made it clear that the "break" had turned into a "break up".

I didn't think I was being too dramatic at the time. I really thought that my life was over then.

I wanted to prove him wrong. That I was the best thing that had ever happened to him, that it was his loss.

One small problem, though. I quickly discovered that casual sex without any strings attached just wasn't my thing.

So after I turned down guy after guy, focusing instead on my classes, desperate to succeed when I'd sacrificed so much for it, I started to fantasize about making Emile beg. Okay, I also fantasized about his eyes, his smile... his mouth, his hands... his amazing dick. Ugh. I fantasized way more than I should have, considering how badly he broke my heart. But mostly I fantasized about being this big success, making him realize he screwed up, making him beg for me to take him back.

I spent a long time fantasizing. Three years almost, while some of my friends who went to Salem State U kept me up to date on his womanizing. It made me sick to hear that Emile was with this girl and that girl, all while I spent every free moment I had either working or with my textbook. Eventually I asked them to stop telling me. I couldn't take it anymore. Emile had his life, I had mine, and somewhere along the way we took different paths.

And then, shortly before Zack got hit by a bus, Emile called me. It was the first phone call in more than two years and it took everything I had to answer it.

He begged. He begged for me to take him back. Just like I'd imagined for years, he begged.

A long distance relationship. He was willing to try if I was.

I told him no.

I've regretted it ever since.

Years. I spent years torturing myself, picturing Emile with one woman, then the next. Wondering what it said about me that, in one breath, he told me he loved me; in the next, he was telling me that we both "needed some space". I stayed away from home—stayed away from my family—all because I was too worried about seeing him again.

Kris's call to apply for the art teacher job was the kick in the ass I needed to get over myself—and to get over Emile. Despite my love of art, working in a gallery had never been for me. I liked getting my hands dirty. Working with kids sounded exciting. Would I throw that opportunity away for a boy I loved when I was eighteen?

I didn't. I wouldn't.

And if I was careful to avoid any of the old haunts in order to keep from running into Emile?

Oops.

I should've known better. Salem was never big enough for the two of us.

Now he wants me to join him in the bathroom stall. There's no way he doesn't mean what I think he means. If Salem isn't big enough for us both, how can a bathroom be?

Last night, when Emile took my hand and led me to my CRV, it was almost like a dream. To have him so casually mention how easy it would be to have a meaningless quickie in a bathroom stall? It's just a reminder of all of the women that came before me.

No, thanks.

All I wanted was another chance at Emile Banks. I never thought I would get it and, now that it's right in front of me—now that *he's* right in front of me—I realize I want more.

Sure, beggars can't be choosers, but I deserve better. A quickie might take the edge off. It's not enough. I need more than that.

I want more than just sex. If that's all he can offer me—if I'm just another warm body to him—I can't do it.

Not again.

6

PROVE ME WRONG

Felicity

EMILE DOESN'T ANSWER ME RIGHT AWAY. FINALLY, WHEN I'm beginning to suspect that he's just going to pretend I didn't say anything at all, he leans back in his seat.

"Why are you surprised? Especially after last night. I can't look at you and not think about sex. I thought you were into it, too. Shit, I hope I wasn't wrong."

He wasn't. I might not have planned what happened in the backseat of my car, but I was definitely into it. Can't find it in me to regret it, either. But that doesn't mean I'm eager to follow him into a stall like who knows how many others.

He's always been a bit of a horndog. I've always been the jealous type.

I guess we didn't change even a little bit.

"You know what? Forget I said anything."

"That's worse than 'nothing, honest'."

"What?"

He shakes his head. "The Felicity I know would finish this conversation without running away from it again."

"Maybe I'm not the Felicity you know anymore, Emile." I try to bring a smile to my face. It comes out more like a grimace. "Five years is a long time. People change. They make new friends, meet new people, sleep around..."

Oops. Did I really say that out loud?

Emile's handsome face closes down, going expressionless.

Yup. Totally did.

"So that's what this is about." He lets out a soft breath, an exhale that has that long strand of hair hanging forward flopping against his forehead. Emile moves forward again, leaning in, keeping his voice low. This discussion is for me and him. "Let's put everything out on the table. I made some mistakes. Had some fun. Met a couple of girls—but that was all after you left."

"Because you dumped me."

"You agreed we needed to take a break."

"You told me we were. What could I say? No? Besides, it doesn't matter. You're grown, Emile. So am I. We made our own choices—"

"How many?"

"Excuse me?"

Emile's jaw is clenched, the edge so sharp I could use it to spread jam on my toast. "Your choices. The guys you met at school. How many?"

"That's none of your business."

"I'll tell you about mine," he offers.

"No, thanks."

A muscle tics in his cheek. "I want to know. Please."

It's the *please* that gets to me.

I know I shouldn't tell him. It really is none of his business and it will only make me feel worse that he knows how pathetic I was while he was busy with any chick that would have him. I don't regret my choices—I'm sitting across from the only regret I've ever had—and if he wants to know so damn bad, I'll tell him.

"None. Okay?"

"None?"

I shrug. "It wasn't because of you or anything. It just... I never had the opportunity."

I'm lying. We both know it.

And that's right about when I realize that I'm in even bigger trouble than I initially thought.

Emile raises one eyebrow. I could never figure out how he did it. I asked him to teach me once, years ago, during a really boring study hall. He laughed at each of my attempts, then pulled some silly faces of his own

59

in order to make me laugh, and we both ended up getting detention for disrupting the class.

Of course, after detention was over, he brought me into the stairwell and fingered me while I kept an eye out for the janitor.

It was the first time we got frisky when there was a risk of someone stumbling upon it. The rush of not knowing when or if we'd be caught heightened the entire experience for me and I actually squealed when Emile made me orgasm in that stairwell.

We christened a nearby hall right before graduation. No one caught us then, either.

In fact, the closest we ever came to being caught was the time Emile's brother, Zack, found us naked in his parents' hot tub. He didn't have any clue that we were—thank god for the bubbles Emile poured inside that kept us hidden—but I refused to do anything when I knew Zack was in the house.

So, of course, I snuck Emile into my house instead. Since my mom and dad lived next door to the Banks' family for years, it made it easy.

Pretending as if I'm not still in love with him after all this time is going to be super fucking hard.

Especially when his entire expression softens as he looks over at me. Before he says a word, Emile reaches across the table, holding out his hand.

I don't take it.

I sigh. "What, Emile? What is it that you want from me?"

He places his hand on the tabletop, palm facing up. It's an invitation I work hard to ignore. "We had this discussion once before. The last time we spoke on the phone. Do you remember?"

I do.

I take a deep breath. This could backfire on me—it has the potential to blow up in my face like a Fourth of July firecracker—but I can't stop myself. "You asked me for a second chance. I told you no."

"You did." He cocks his head, a shadow flashing across his face. I can't get a read on him at that moment. He straightens, pulling his hand back, settling it in his lap. A smile tugs on his perfect lips. "I haven't changed my mind."

Time stops.

So *that's* what this is about. It's not just sex, is it? He's still trying to convince me to give him another shot.

And I want to.

I really, really do.

I know I shouldn't. My sister is gonna lecture the shit out of me later on. It'll be worth it, too.

One last try. This time, if I say no, I'll look back on this moment and regret it for the rest of my life.

"Okay. Look. I might be willing to change my mind—"

His whole face brightens. A heartbeat later, his expression turns wolfish. "Felicity, I—"

"—but I won't sleep with you," I add, cutting back in when Emile tries to interrupt me. "Not yet, anyway."

His strong jaw hangs for a second before closing with an audible *click*. He blinks. "No sex."

I shake my head.

"And you're serious?"

I nod.

He pauses, letting my condition run through his brain. "What if I don't agree?"

"Then I'm sure I'll see you around. Thanks for breakfast. The jam was delicious."

His dark brown eyes go impossibly darker. Beneath the restaurant's fluorescent lights, they almost appear black. "You really think so little of me. I'm hurt, Felicity."

Too bad. I pick my mug up again, draining the last of my now-cool coffee. "Yeah? Prove me wrong."

"I might just do that."

"You don't have to if you don't want to."

"I want to," he says quickly, shoving his plate away before placing his elbows on the tabletop. He leans into me, all humor suddenly gone. "You already set your terms. No sex. Fine. I wasn't kidding last night when I said I missed your taste, but it's not the only thing I missed. You're back, Felicity. Whatever you want from me, you'll get it. So long as I get to have you."

Whoa.

That was, uh... whoa.

He's so serious. And forceful. And *hot*.

Oh, man.

I never thought he would agree. Emile Banks was supposed to laugh it off, thank me for joining him for breakfast, then argue over whose turn it was to pay. That's the boy I remembered. The man who is so willing to readily do what I say instead of trying to talk me out of it? He's new.

And I really, really think I like him.

Well, I've already come this far. He wants me? Okay. He's got to earn it.

"We date."

"What?"

"Dates," I say again. "We go out. We get to know each other again. No sex until we both agree that we're ready to take that step. How's that sound?"

Emile thinks it over for a second before nodding. "I can do that."

Emile

I can't do that.

What was I thinking?

Sitting across from Felicity, gazing at her pretty

face, watching her lick her lips after every bite of bacon she takes... okay, so maybe I wasn't thinking.

Can you blame me?

Felicity Houston is temptation incarnate. If I thought I could get away with it, I would take her right here on the table. Something about the jealous way she kept eyeing the server waiting on our table got me going. I thought I was good for not mentioning the bathrooms until she'd finished eating. It was certainly on my mind throughout our entire meal.

It wasn't until Felicity lost her smile, her big blue eyes boring holes into the table as if it had personally offended her, that I realized my goof.

Didn't matter that it's been two years since I've been with anyone. Felicity has gone five years—and I was her last.

I never expected that. I shouldn't be so pleased to know that but, shit, that's the best thing I ever heard.

Of course, then she had to go on and tell me that we could date. That's definitely a win. But no sex?

After that taste of heaven last night?

I had to agree. What else could I do? That's her dealbreaker, and my stubborn Felicity has made her mind up. No force on earth is going to get her to change it. I guess I should just be grateful that she's even giving me the chance to date her again.

I've got no one to blame but myself. God, I was a fucking moron. How did I ever think that my fun with other girls wouldn't get back to Felicity? It's not like New Jersey is on the other side of the planet or something. Half our graduating class ended up at Salem State U. Of course she would've been tuned into the gossip grapevine.

But I'm different now. I'm not the reckless kid who thought with his dick instead of his brain. I already accepted ages ago that I fucked up big time by letting Felicity slip away from me. If keeping my dick in my pants until she's ready for it is all she asks of me, I'll have to live with it.

Besides, it isn't like I've been getting laid on the regular anyway. Ever since I set my sights on winning this woman back into my arms—and my bed—I haven't even thought about sleeping with anyone else. Having her so close, the memory of her taste still lingering on my tongue... it's gonna suck.

But I'll do it.

I have to.

7

TWO WORDS

Felicity

MY PLAN MIGHT HAVE BACKFIRED ON ME JUST A SCOOCH.

Emile has been a perfect gentleman since our breakfast date. He doesn't push. He follows my lead. He's following my condition to the letter.

And he's getting on my last nerve.

I know I can't complain. He's only doing what I asked him to do. It's crazy. Even though he's been out of my life for the last five years—his doing, I keep reminding myself when it's clear I'm falling even harder than before—we go together so perfectly that it's like he never broke up with me and I never left. He's as easy for me to read today as he was when he was younger. I know what he's thinking before he's even thinking it.

Emile is ready to burst. If I didn't feel like I was ready to explode from sexual tension myself, I would've considered it poetic justice.

It's been two weeks since I insisted that we keep sex on the back burner. I can admit now that I was a little bitter about how easy it was for Emile to talk me into our little interlude on the Fourth when I came up with that condition. Not that I don't still think it's a good idea. For my own sanity and self-esteem, I needed to know that Emile wanted to rekindle our relationship because he wanted to see *me* again and not just fuck me.

He wants to do that, too. I'm more than aware of it. Every time we're together—and it's been just about every moment he's free from work that he wants to be with me—I see him watching me, lust fueling his expression. He wants to get in my panties so bad, he's got to be walking around with the bluest balls in all of Salem.

But he hasn't acted on it. Not once. The most we've done is make out like we're back to being teenagers again. Whenever I make a move to go one step further, though, Emile forces himself to stop.

I love him for it as much as I want to strangle him.

A girl's got needs. I went five years mainly ignoring them because I missed Emile and it just didn't seem right being with anyone else. I kept telling myself that the right guy would come along and he would bang the memory of Emile right out of my head. It just... it never happened.

Now I only want Emile to bang me and help me forget what it was like to be without him.

I don't know how long I'll have him this time around. In the last two weeks, I've gotten to know this newer, older, surprisingly more mature Emile; dealing with Zack's unfortunate accident had done what I hadn't thought anything would: it made Emile grow up.

But I haven't fooled myself into believing that his feelings about long-term relationships have changed, no matter how many times he tried to insist that they have. When he proposed the idea of a "break", when he ended what we had, he made it clear that he didn't plan on getting tied down again. He said he was doing that for me, giving me space to find myself while I went away to school. Even then I knew it was bullshit. The truth was that we were eighteen, we'd only ever been with each other, and Emile wanted to see what was out there.

I don't know what he found. I don't want to. But I do know—because Emile made a point to tell me—that he hasn't been with anyone in more than two years. Seeing his brother in a coma, inches away from death, had triggered something in Emile. Zack is okay now, he's married and expecting a kid, but Emile's whole perspective on life has obviously switched.

He says he's looking for forever, then he takes my hand. He holds it tight, giving it a squeeze. It's sweet. And I want to believe him.

Not that it matters when I don't. I've decided that he might still be completely full of shit, but I'm helpless to do anything except succumb to it.

He says forever. I'm not holding out hope for more than this summer. If that's all I'll get out of Emile this time around, why am I wasting precious moments by pushing him away when all I really want to do is hold him close?

Something has to change. With Emile only doing what I've asked of him, I know it's gotta be up to me.

That's fine.

I know exactly what I'm going to do. And if Emile knows me as well as I do him, he shouldn't be too surprised by what I have in mind.

Just as I have that thought, turning myself on as I imagine Emile's expression when he figures out what I've got planned for tonight, my phone rings. It's tucked under my towel so that it's out of the direct sunlight. I slip my hand beneath it, snatch the phone, then answer it.

"Hello?"

Emile's voice filters in through the speaker. "Felicity, babe. Miss me?"

Two words. That's all it takes. And maybe I'm too close to being combustible, depriving myself when I know Emile would give me what I want if I just broke down and asked for it, but those two words have me clenching my thighs together.

"Depends."

"Yeah? On what?"

"On how much you miss me."

"Oh, baby, you have no idea." His answer is swift, and if I didn't know better, I would think he actually means it. "I'm counting down the minutes until I can see you again."

"Movie's at nine," I tell him. "You'll see me then."

"I can't wait that long. I get out at six. I'll swing by Kris's and get you by quarter after."

Emile never asks. It used to drive me nuts when I was younger. A headstrong teen who thought she knew everything, I hated it when Emile would pull that *I'm three months older, I know better* bullshit.

Now, though? His take-charge attitude is kind of hot, and if he's so desperate to see me that he's telling me that he's picking me up right after he gets out of work, I'm into it. To be honest, I'm dying to see him, too.

Still, I can't let him know that. Right now I have the upper-hand. It won't last, but I'll take it for as long as I can.

"I should be ready by then. We'll see."

Emile lets out a short, disbelieving laugh. Probably because I might have said *We'll see.* The breathiness in my voice, though? That all but screams *Take me now*.

Who knows? If everything goes according to plan—

"You'll be ready," he says, sounding assured. "What're you doing now, beautiful?"

He called me 'beautiful'. Not the first time, either. I still have a hard time believing he's serious when I think about the frickin' Adonis Emile transformed into. It does something to the pit of my stomach every time he says it, too.

Clearing my throat, glad he can't see the way I'm flushing, I tell him, "Nothing much. Just sitting by the pool, waiting for you to get out of work."

Emile's low rasp of a chuckle washes over me. "Skinnydipping?"

"I wish, but Kris is home with the kids." I purposely let regret color my words, grinning when he barely stifles his groan. I can't help myself. I laugh. "What's wrong, Emile? Thinking of my boobs?"

"And other parts of you," he murmurs. "You just got me hard as a rock, Felicity, and I have to walk into a meeting in about two minutes. That wasn't fair."

"All's fair in love and war."

"Yeah? What do we have going on right now?"

Good question. "I'll leave that for you to figure out."

"Yeah, if I survive this meeting. Not kidding, babe.

If I'm not careful, I could poke my boss's eye out with my dick."

Good. I'm glad. If just the thought of me topless is enough to get him going, he'll never be able to resist what I have in mind tonight.

"Sorry." I'm so not sorry. "Hey, if you do survive, we still good for this weekend?"

Kris, Dave, and the girls are going away for the weekend. Even though she's still a little annoyed at me for spending all of my free time with Emile after what he put me through, she's supporting me. Didn't stop her from trying to get me to come along on their family trip. I felt weird, staying behind, and with Emile taking me out every night, I didn't want to go with them and lose a single second with him. So I asked him if he had any idea what I should do and, since he's Emile Banks, of course he did.

We're supposed to be heading out early tomorrow morning together, a trip just for us. Emile thinks I booked us a hotel in upstate New Hampshire, where we can hike and hang out and just continue to get to know each other again.

I didn't book the hotel.

I have no intention of leaving Salem.

Because, honestly, I'm not too sure I really need to get to know Emile. Maybe he did change in a couple of notable ways. At his core, though? He's not so different. I'm pretty sure I know Emile.

After tonight, I'm willing to bet he'll be glad to stay behind.

"Wha— oh, of course. Yeah. It'll be a challenge, staying the night with you and stopping at cuddling. You're so damn tempting, Felicity. But it'll be... it'll be fun."

Fun. Right. I have to work hard to swallow my giggle. He sounds so tortured.

But then he goes on to add, "Besides, you think I'm gonna miss a chance to show you how much I want this? I won't fuck this up again, Felicity. Hone—I mean, yeah. Me and you. Until you say so, my nights are yours," and I decide then and there that I've had enough of making both of us wait.

Because what he should have said was his *evenings*. His nights? They've probably been as lonely as mine.

They *better* be as lonely as mine.

Emile Banks belongs to me. I feel confident enough to admit that now. And, okay, maybe I did let him walk away from me once. *Until you say so...* it's only been two weeks, I get that, but it doesn't matter. I was a goner the moment he popped up unannounced at my face-painting booth. If it's up to me, I'll give him the forever he keeps claiming he's after. If it's up to me—

But that's it. It's never been up to me.

Whatever. It's fine. He's here now, and if he's going to leave again? It's not like I'll be surprised. Until then, for as long as I can keep him, for as long as he'll stay, I

74

want to give him everything I have, take everything he'll offer in return. He owes me.

Then, maybe, when he leaves me again, I'll know it wasn't for a lack of trying on my part.

And I'll have fresh memories to cling to when I'm back to fantasizing alone at night.

EMILE LIKED TO TAKE CHARGE. IT'S ALWAYS BEEN ONE BIG facet of his overbearing personality. He's forever been convinced that he knows best and, since I usually am pretty easygoing until someone gives me a reason not to be, I let him take the lead. It worked for us because, when I really pushed for something, Emile would back down.

Once we arrive at the movie theater, I pointedly tell the clerk that I want two tickets to the action movie playing in the next fifteen minutes. It's been out for weeks and was a pretty big bust compared to some of the more recent films.

Before I started to see Emile again, I had no intention of ever sitting through it. Now? It's perfect for what I have in mind. It's dark, it's loud, and it's been out for a while so there's a good chance that we'll be alone in there.

Emile doesn't stop me from ordering the tickets. I'm sure he's confused. We both talked about it the other day and decided to see the new rom-com that came out last week.

Hey, what can I say? A lady reserves the right to be fickle.

Once I paid for the tickets—this is my idea and I insisted—we head toward the back of the movie theater. They put our movie in the second-to-last theater in the whole place so it's a bit of a walk. Good. I need a little more time to work up my nerve.

Emile has his arm slung over my shoulder, tucking me into his side. He takes the ticket stub I hold out to him, reading the tiny print.

"You sure you want to see this movie, babe? There's like three summer blockbusters that came out this week alone. I'm surprised this one's still even playing."

"I'm sure."

He narrows his dark eyes down on me. "The Felicity I knew used to hate action movies."

She still does. "I heard good things about this one."

Right. Like how there are so many explosions, half the people walked out of it complaining that their ears were ringing. And it's kind of short. Perfect. I won't have to sit through a lot of it before it gets right to the action.

Then I can get right to the action.

I'm super relieved to discover that my prayers have been answered. No one else is sitting in the theater. It's one of the smaller ones, too, and it just seems that much more intimate. Just in case, I steer Emile towards a row further in the back.

When he raises his eyebrow, I shrug. "We've got the entire to ourselves. Might as well get cozy."

"I like cozy."

He's gonna like what I have planned even more.

The multiplex is a more of an old-fashioned movie theater: creaky, cramped seats, sticky floor, and speakers that are loud as fuck. I chose this one instead of the fancy dine-in one on the other side of town for a couple of reasons. First, because there's definitely less people who come in here now. Second, because there's no servers that interrupt you as you're trying to watch a movie. And, most importantly, because me and Emile had one of our first dates here.

I know he remembers that as well as I do. When I said I wanted to go to the movies, he didn't even question my choice. This will always be our movie theater. We have so many memories here.

About fifteen minutes into the movie, I work up the nerve to begin building more.

I'm not surprised that Emile is totally into the film. This is right up his alley, with the smoking hot leads, unnecessary explosions, and a world that's heading for the apocalypse. He's holding my hand loosely in his, always keeping that tether between us, but his focus is for the getaway scene up on the screen.

Here goes nothing.

I slip my hand out of his. *That* gets his attention.

"What are you doing?" he whispers.

I pretend not to hear him. Slowly, easily, I reach over and tap the button on his jeans. It takes a second —it's super dark and I'm more nervous than I thought I would be—but I manage to flick his jeans open on my second try. I reach for the zipper pull.

Emile doesn't ask again. He knows exactly what I'm doing.

Or, rather, he *thinks* he does.

An anticipatory grin flashes across his face. The movie is immediately forgotten as Emile relaxes into his seat, spreading his legs just enough to give me room.

I look closer. No. Relax... that isn't quite right. Glancing down, I notice that he's gripping the arm rest between us so tightly, I wouldn't be surprised if it snaps right off.

Good.

I slowly begin to tug on his zipper.

8

CAN I?

Emile

I'VE NEVER HEARD ANYTHING LOUDER IN MY LIFE THAN the sound of my zipper as Felicity tugs it down. It seems to echo all around us, even drowning out the explosions coming from the screen.

She hesitates, her fingers so close that I swear I can feel their heat through my boxers. I have this insane urge to take her hand in mine, then slip it inside my open jeans. I don't want to scare her or rush her or give her any damn reason to stop what she's doing so I don't.

I don't know what the hell she's doing, but I know I don't want her to stop.

I've been waiting weeks for her to make a move. Is it finally time? I hope so.

Her fingers twitch, barely brushing the edge of the zipper treads. What's going on? Felicity isn't a tease, so why—

"Can I?" she murmurs.

Ah. So *that's* why. Just like how I gave her the chance to back out on the Fourth of July, she's waiting for me to give her the go sign. This is really happening. After telling me we had to wait to be intimate, she's actually initiating some kind of sex with me. I'm sure of it.

And I'm suddenly afraid to say anything, like if I open my mouth, the wrong thing will pop out and she'll stop what she's doing. So I just nod. Yes, Felicity. Fucking yes.

She gets the message. A split second later, she reaches inside of my jeans, her fingers landing lightly on the head of my cock. Her hand is so, so soft.

And I'm instantly hard.

Felicity circles the head with light strokes. I let out a low groan.

"Shh. You have to stay quiet."

Stay quiet? She's kidding, right?

Gulping, I nod again. My fingers dig into the arm rests but hell if I make a single peep as she grabs my cock, feeding it through the open gap in my jeans. It's not such a reach that she'd do this in the middle of the movies. We're the only ones in the whole showing, so it's not like anyone can see us, though there's always a chance a late straggler might show up, or an usher might poke their head in.

It's what always made it so exciting for Felicity. Only... she wanted to wait.

Maybe we've waited long enough?

My body belongs to her, just like my heart always has. She wants to give me handjob rather than pay attention to the screen? I'm down. She never has to ask me if she can touch me. And if she wants me to stay quiet, I'd rather swallow my tongue than disappoint her again.

"Don't move," she whispers before giving my whole length, root to tip, one leisurely stroke.

Does it count that my dick jerks against her palm all on its own, desperate for her touch? I sure as hell hope not. Don't move. That one might just be asking a little too much.

She lets go.

I want to fucking bawl.

I made the decision, though, when I agreed to Felicity's whole "no sex" thing two weeks ago. She wanted to take it slow, see if what we have between us is more than intense attraction and a need to bone whenever we get close. I get it. And she was right.

Absence makes the heart grow fonder, right? Seems like *abstinence* does the same. Without the distraction of sex, I discovered that I'm still as madly, hopelessly, stupidly in love with Felicity Houston as I was when I let my fear of our future together talk me into pushing her away.

Her chair squeaks. Keeping her head ducked, Felicity gets out of her seat, then immediately drops to her knees. I hear a faint crinkling sound that's immediately lost in the echoes of gunfight coming from the big screen. Her head is still lowered, zeroing in on my twitching cock.

She presses one kiss to the head.

Stay quiet.

Don't move.

If she gives me a blowjob in the middle of the multiplex while I'm this pent-up, it's gonna be a testament to how much I want to prove myself to Felicity if I manage to do what she wants me to do. Then again, there isn't a single thing in this world I *wouldn't* do just to get her lush lips wrapped around my cock.

It doesn't happen.

I feel something on my cock, though. With one quick motion, Felicity slips some latex on me, rolling it all the way up.

A condom?

Is that a condom?

"What are you—?"

Felicity puts her finger to her lips. "Shh."

Shit. Stay quiet.

A light flashes on the screen. Another explosion. It

gives me enough light to peek down and check. Yup. That's a condom all right.

What the—

A condom for some head? Does that even make sense? I mean, I'd have to be an even bigger moron not to realize that my past hurt her more than I thought it would. But it's been years since I was with anyone else and I've been tested. I'm clean. Even if she didn't want to hear it, I made sure Felicity knew that—

Felicity stands up. Another flash on the screen. I'm not even paying attention to the movie anymore. The flash is helpful, though. It lights up the absolutely devilish look on Felicity's face the moment before she turns her back, lifts her skirt, and reveals that she's not wearing any panties underneath.

Call me slow. Don't care. Maybe all the blood rushed straight to my dick, leaving none for my brain. For a second, I stare up at her in confusion. She doesn't know. She can't see me. And thank god for that because, a second later when she firmly grasps my cock in her hand before pressing the tip to her pussy, I realize that it should've been fucking obvious.

I go absolutely still. Don't move. That's what she said. If it kills me, I'm gonna stay motionless until I'm balls deep inside of her.

It takes a few minutes. I'm not all that small and it's been a while for Felicity. She takes her time adjusting to my cock, wiggling just enough to make me grit my teeth as she slowly sinks down. I don't rush her. This was her idea and I want this so bad, I won't risk anything messing it up.

And then, with a soft gasp of surprise, she's done. I'm completely inside of her.

I never want to leave.

Burying my face in her back, I let out a much louder groan than before. I couldn't help myself. The warmth, the heat, the absolute vice that is her pussy as she fully seats herself on my lap... this is it. This is heaven. Heaven is leaning back in a movie seat, the most gorgeous woman I've ever seen sitting on top of me, my cock buried so deeply that I can't tell where she begins or I end. We're the best part of being together and, holy shit, she's starting to move.

Slow at first, as if she's getting used to me stretching her out, but it's not long before she finds a rhythm that has my eyes just about rolling to the back of my head.

Her ass slaps against my jeans. The denim is a great muffler. Skin hitting skin makes a distinct, loud sound, but her ass against the fabric is barely noticeable as she lifts, falls, lifts, falls, working me so hard, so fast, that it's only been a few minutes and my balls are growing heavy with their need to nut.

I hold on. What kind of lover would I be if I just let myself go without taking care of Felicity first? She might have made the first move, but that only means that she's opening the door for me to do what I've wanted to do for a long, long time.

After grabbing her hips, helping her set a pace that has us both panting with need, I use my left hand to support her as she continues to fuck me hard. My right hand snakes around to her front.

Her skirt is flapping in time to the rhythm of her riding me. Timing it perfectly, I slip my hand under the bunched up material, finding her pussy easily. It's dark, I'm definitely distracted now, but I'm one determined bastard. My fingers hit the bump and the top of her mound, moving with her as she bounces. Up down, up down. Knowing where her clit is now, I keep my hand cupped over her pussy as she rides, my fingers probing her folds until I find the little pearl.

And then I start to rub it in time to our frantic coupling.

It doesn't take long for Felicity to get off. Between the risk of being out in the open, the way she keeps fucking herself on my cock, and the way I work her clit, she's coming within minutes.

Sweat breaks out on my forehead. I pump faster while struggling to hold back my own nut. Felicity first.

For me, it's about Felicity first.

As it should have always been.

As it *will* be—

I can't stop myself from grinning when I hear that familiar squeal, followed by the spasms of her pussy as she comes all over my cock. I steal a kiss against her neck, then murmur, "Shh. Gotta be quiet, babe."

I really am a bit of an asshole. At least Felicity gets it. She chuckles, swallows another squeal, then squeezes me so hard the next time she's sitting that I can't stop myself from coming.

Grabbing her hips again, holding her flush against me as I thrust all of the way up inside of her, I fill that whole fucking condom before I'm done riding out my orgasm. Even then, when my cock finally manages to go limp enough to slide easily out of her, I keep her on my lap. She's still panting and I feel like I'm ready for a good, long nap—and then, maybe, another round of sex—but there's nothing like this feeling of content-ment as she snuggles into me before finally admitting in a breathless whisper, "I missed that, Emile. But not more than I missed you."

My heart starts to beat triple-time.

The dates were the beginning. The sex was just as great as I remembered, if not better. But to have Felicity finally—*finally*—admit to me that she missed me while she was gone... hell fucking yes.

This is the only win I need.

Because Felicity really is home now.

She's mine, too.

And I'm never, ever letting her go.

9

LOVE FINDS A WAY

Emile

I'M AS GOOD AS MY WORD.

I bring Felicity home with me that night. There isn't even a question about dropping her back off at her sister's place. As soon as the credits begin to roll, I grab her by the hand, desperate to get back inside of her again. Felicity's delighted laughter is music to my ears, second only to her soft pants and squeals of pleasure whenever I make her come.

Screw the hiking trip. We don't leave my bedroom the whole weekend, and after I make her come twice in a row, Felicity confesses that she had hoped that this would be how we spent my days off. That little minx.

God, I fucking love her.

On Monday, after I get home from work, I just

come out and ask her if she'd like to move in with me instead of continuing her pointless search for a home of her own in Salem. After she pretends to die from shock that I *asked* instead of simply telling her she was moving in, she puts me out of my misery and says she can be moved in by Friday.

I call Zack. He calls his brother-in-law, Dani's brother Max, and the three of us have Felicity's stuff packed up and moved into my place before Wednesday morning.

I'm no fool. I lost her once. It was the biggest fucking mistake I made in my entire life. And, sure, maybe the time apart was something we needed considering how hard and how fast we fell as kids, but I had all the time I needed. Never again.

We spend the entire summer together. I help Felicity study for and eventually pass the exam so that her job at Salem High is secured. She's my date to Dani's baby shower, then to Max's mid-August wedding to his sweetheart of a fiance, Allison. We take a week's vacation together out to Martha's Vineyard, booking a room at a quaint bed and breakfast where we missed breakfast more often than not, but got our money's worth out of the bed

We go to the movies whenever we can and our streak of getting off without getting caught continues.

In September, Felicity starts her job at Salem High. I wait with bated breath to make sure she loves it. It's the reason why she came back so it's important to me because it's so damn important to her. Besides, what if she hates it? It's not like I don't know that she could return to her fancy gallery gig in a heartbeat if she wants to. Her boss has sent like four pleading e-mails to Felicity, asking her to return. She says she won't, but I don't realize how much I have riding on her liking her job as an art teacher until she closes out her first week and gleefully tells me that she believes she has finally found her calling.

I found mine in a buxom blonde with deceptively innocent blue eyes and a wicked streak a mile long.

Heading into October, three months after I found Felicity at the Fourth of July festivities, I decide it's time to do something about it.

WHEN ZACK SURPRISED US WITH THE NEWS THAT HE WAS engaged to a woman within weeks of his escape from the rehab center, I have to admit that I thought the coma had done something funny to his head. My brother is ten years older than me, and he'd never showed any sign that he was interested in keeping one woman around for the long haul.

As his brother, it was up to me to throw his bachelor's party. Most of Zack's friends had a hard time knowing what to say after his accident so I kept it low key: just me, Zack, and Max heading out to a local bar for some beers and an *I can't believe you're really doing this* night out on the town. After seeing the way Zack absolutely doted on Dani, I knew there was no talking him out of it.

What did surprise me, though?

How, with six beers in him, Zack looked me dead in the eye and told me, clear as day, that love finds a way. He was a little wasted at that point—he was still recovering and his tolerance was shit—and he started saying something about Halloween and ghosts that I didn't quite get since I was about four beers deep myself, but Zack was adamant that when you find love, you do whatever you have to in order to hold onto it.

I thought I understood that part. I didn't—not until I saw that fateful post back in July and I saw my happily-ever-after staring back at me.

I bought the ring three weeks after Felicity moved into my place. I kept it hidden in the glove compartment of my car, waiting for the right moment to give it to her. Zack was right when he said that love finds a way. Felicity, however, climbed into my bed every night, then woke up the next morning as if she was surprised to find that I was still there. Until I could convince her that I had no intention of giving her up again, giving her the ring would be just another promise she would expect me to break.

One crisp night in October, as Felicity leaned into

me, discussing plans for Halloween, then Thanksgiving, for Christmas, for New Years... for the future as if she had finally accepted that *we* would have one... that's when I knew it was time.

As soon as she told me how much she enjoyed her new job, I moved the ring into our bedroom. I kept it buried at the bottom of my sock drawer. Excusing myself, pausing to steal a quick kiss before I climb off of the couch, I promise Felicity that I would be right back.

I return less than a minute later, the ring box nestled in the center of my palm.

Her eyes go wide when she catches sight of it. Slowly, carefully, she leans forward as if the small, velvet box is drawing her near. "Emile... what is that?"

She has to know. I see hope written on her beautiful features, a yearning that she only has for me. Even if I wasn't positive before this, that look sealed it.

Maybe we're moving too fast. Maybe I still have a lot to do to prove myself. I don't give a shit.

I'm terrified that Felicity will realize she can do so much better than me. Call me a selfish prick—my sweet Felicity certainly has, and so much worse, I'm sure—but if she doesn't realize that yet, I'm locking her up before she gets the chance.

"It's simple. When you feel the spark, when you know it's right, you follow your gut." I open the box, revealing the engagement ring I picked out for her. "And you follow your heart."

Felicity lets out a breathy giggle. Her voice is almost shaking as she cracks out a response. "Well, that's definitely a sparkler you got there."

"I know we're young. And you might think we're rushing things. I don't. And, hey, my parents were married and had Zack by the time they were twenty-three. I went five years without you, Felicity. I don't want to spend another minute wondering if you'll find someone better. I want to make you mine so that I never try to give you your space again."

She sucks in a breath of air. I don't think she expected me to come out and add that last part. I had to, though. It's the elephant inside of the room with us at all times. Jeez, I really was a selfish prick. I "gave her space" to go away to Rutgers because that's what I wanted.

I guess I didn't change after all. Proposing to Felicity after only dating for three months this time around, putting my wants before her needs again—

And that's when Felicity stands up.

I freeze, the ring box still offered out to her as she closes in on me.

"I would've married you at eighteen." She looks up at me, her big baby blues gone even wider. Her mouth parts, her tongue slipping through the gap in her teeth as she pauses, choosing her next words carefully. "If you would've asked me straight after graduation, I would've said yes. And it would've been an awful mistake."

That's, uh, not really what I wanted to hear. It wasn't a no—I'm not even sure it was an answer at all. But 'mistake'. She definitely said 'mistake'. Shit.

Too soon. I proposed too soon.

"Felicity—"

"I'm twenty-three," she continues, cutting me off. "I've moved out of Salem, I've lived on my own, I've seen what the world has to offer. In the end, I came back home. I belong here." She hesitates, and when she tilts her head back so that she's looking deep in my eyes, I see the truth here. I don't need to make this woman mine.

She already is.

"Marry me, Felicity," I whisper.

"When you feel it, you know," she whispers back. "The spark never died, not for me, not ever. Give me the ring."

My heart just about stops. *Give me the ring*. I snatch the damn thing out of its box so fast, the band nearly cuts into the underside of my finger. I start to hold it out, hesitating because, damn it, I have to be sure.

"Wait— so... it's a yes?"

"It's a hell yes, Emile." Felicity's eyes sparkle. "You think I could find someone else to put up with my exhibitionist streak?"

She sticks her hand out. Before she changes her mind, I quickly slide the engagement ring on her all important finger.

It's a perfect fit.

Just like the two of us.

AUTHOR'S NOTE

Thank you for reading *When Sparks Fly*!

So that's it. The end of the *Holiday Hunk* series. I can hardly believe it, but since each book kind of led to the next, I feel like this is a perfect stopping point. Ever since Zack woke up out of his coma in the first book (*Halloween Boo*) and found his younger brother, Emile, there to tell him all about his time in the coma, I knew I wanted to give Emile a story of his own. The mention of the next door neighbor in the hot tub? It's just what I needed. This book is a little different from the last couple in the series—there's no magic, for one—but I feel like I've come full circle with it.

Which is why I've decided to finish this series with six books. I do want to take the time to thank everyone who took a chance on me, reading these strange and steamy romantic novellas that were born out of my life-long obsession with *Hocus Pocus*.

Up next: I'm going to tackle shifters! So keep scrolling for a blurb and the cover.

Until then, I hope you enjoyed *When Sparks Fly*! Make sure to join my newsletter or like my facebook page to keep up to date on my next release.

— Sarah

AVAILABLE NOW

NEVER HIS MATE

After my mate rejected me, I wanted to kill him. Instead, I ran away—which nearly killed *me*...

A year ago, everything was different. I had just left my home, joining the infamous Mountainside Pack. The daughter of an omega wolf, I've always been prized -- but just not as prized as I would be if my new packmates found out my secret.

But then my fated mate—Mountainside's Alpha—rejects me in front of his whole pack council and my secret gets out, I realize I only have one option. Going lone wolf is the only choice I've got, and I take it.

97

Now I live in Muncie, hiding in plain sight. If the wolves ever left the mountains surrounding the city, I'd be in big trouble. Luckily, the truce between the vampires and my people is shaky at best and Muncie? It's total vamp territory. Thanks to my new vamp roomie, I get a pass, and I try to forget all about the call of the wolf. It's tough, though. I... I just can't forget my embarrassment—and my anger—from that night.

And then *he* shows up and my chance at forgetting flies out the damn wind.

Ryker Wolfson. He was supposed to be my fated mate, but he chose his pack over our bond. At least, he did—but now that he knows what I've been hiding, he wants me back.

But doesn't he remember?

I told him I'll never be his mate, and there isn't a single thing he can do to change my mind.

To Ryker, that sounds like a challenge. And if there's one thing I know about wolf shifters, it's that they can never resist a challenge.

Just like I'm finding it more difficult than I should to resist *him*.

---

* ***Never His Mate*** is the first novel in the *Claw and Fang* series. It's a steamy rejected mates shifter romance, and though the hero eventually realizes his mistake, the fierce, independent heroine isn't the sweet wolf everyone thinks she's supposed to be...

Get it now!

KEEP IN TOUCH

Stay tuned for what's coming up next! Sign up for my mailing list for news, promotions, upcoming releases, and more!

Sarah Spade's Stories

And make sure to check out my Facebook page for all release news:

http://facebook.com/sarahspadebooks

Sarah Spade is a pen name that I used specifically to write these holiday-based novellas (as well as a few books that will be coming out in the future). If you're interested in reading other books that I've written (romantic suspense, Greek mythology-based romance, shifters/vampires/witches romance, and fae romance), check out my other author account here:

http://amazon.com/author/jessicalynch

ALSO BY SARAH SPADE

Holiday Hunks

Halloween Boo

This Christmas

Auld Lang Mine

I'm With Cupid

Getting Lucky

When Sparks Fly

Holiday Hunk: the Complete Series

Claws and Fangs

Leave Janelle

Never His Mate

Always Her Mate

Forever Mates

Hint of Her Blood

Claws Clause

(written as Jessica Lynch)

Mates *free*

Hungry Like a Wolf

Of Mistletoe and Mating

No Way

Season of the Witch

Rogue

Sunglasses at Night

Ain't No Angel *free*

True Angel

Ghost of Jealousy

Night Angel

Broken Wings

Lost Angel

Born to Run

Ordinance 7304: Books 1-3

Printed in Great Britain
by Amazon